# Pushing Poetry

## E.I. Karnes

PUSHING POETRY. Copyright © 2014, 2015, 2017, 2020, 2021
Photograph, Designed & Published by E. I. Karnes
Editor-in-Chief: M. W. Karnes.
Copyeditor: M. A. Meholick
Published 2023. All rights reserved.

Second Edition

ISBN: 979-8-9876650-0-8

Library of Congress Control Number: 2023901449

Pine Grove
Pennsylvania

Other Books
by E. I. Karnes

Makes Murky Waters Sparkle

# Dedication Page

Dr. & Mrs. Pifer
Mom & Dad
My Nephews
Challengers
My Boss
My Godfather
Dana
Myself
ChrisP

# Contents

## Pushing Poetry

da da da da da da da, da da da da da

## 501 is Calling

A single tree stands to block your view,
But only a few centimeters of the whole.

Looking into the vast opening
A bird flies by, usually above, but now below.

A path has lead to this wonderful oasis
Only to lead on again and carry me away

To another awaiting place.

Future In Your Eyes


Hear the wonderful breeze whispering to me.
Hear the wind whispering your name through the trees and
As I grow I know it's true
Your love is so beautiful too.

Hear my footsteps fall upon the ground and
Know that I know that you're always around
To see me as I look your way,
So pure a soul you stay.

When deer cross upon my path,
I know that things are better left in the past and as
I see into your honest eyes,
I see the future. Surprise!

When I think about you,
I know that there's a future staring back at me.
You and I will always be true,
The sky knows it too.

## The Trip

A rewarding sunrise with the moon still visible was at the end of a long, night drive to Lake Erie.

Sapphire waters now topped with the morning light rolled with colors of lit coal and ebbed at our feet along the otherwise vacant shore.

Atop a forbidden rock wall styled tide breaker the view laid endlessly upon the freshwater horizon.

A picnic table opposite the texture of driftwood, partially consumed by sand, seared by the sun and burnt black at spots (proving that it survived fire), served its purpose well as I sat and waited for the sun to raise the air temperature to match the warmth of the water.

Green foliage that speckled the dunes was now visible and alive with the light of the morning, as it was dark on the way in, while I teetered through the sand and looked forward to the rest of the trip.

## Moon Mood

There goes the lion,
Virgin hot on his tail.
I'm fire tending
Spending my time
Waiting for the moon.

You might think me lazy,
A little crazy too,
But that's on you.
Who's to say
I'm not in the mood?

## Eclipse

Write me a song,
Not looking up,
Not feeling down,
Eyes are on the ground.

Wait a moment—
It's not a cloud,
It's the eclipse coming 'round

Must some eyes
Never mend:
Our human flaws
We defend.

Pillow Beach

The sea lies
Lapping on Pillow Beach.

Tossing and turning,
Shells and sand,

Rest so far from deep.

Stars on the horizon:
It's dark

So see that in dream
Water and land nap together.

Behind the Clouds


I mourn roadkill and follow speed limits.
I often gaze at puddles of water to see the sky.

Occasionally the sun is visible
Even when it lies behind clouds,

Which at times cannot be seen
Looking up with the naked eye.

From the Heart


I've got my music and I've got my open heart.
There is nothing more I could ask for, what a great start.
I'm a good person, you might wonder why.
Just listen to my story, it will tell you I

Will not sink in the lows of life,
Grow when I can and
See the world through open eyes
As they are even closed.

I accept the things I know,
Know what I don't and
The things that I don't understand
I'll let go like grains of sand.

I've got my mind set on peace and I know where to start.
The way things are today love will set you apart.
Don't forget about the little things; don't ponder too much.
Just listen to my story, it will tell you

Might be best to sit and listen, not walk on by.
Understand knowledge gained is just a piece of the pie.
Keep your mind open. Don't close any doors.
Be entertained by mine, it will tell you I—

# Gute Nacht

Walking barefoot in the snow,
Having gone up away from the low,
I have my days in the evening,
Making sense of feelings and just believing
Everyday is a good day.

News


Wonderful thoughts abound
So I formulate words to get them off the ground

In hopes that they'll turn into adamant feelings
That can easily be found.

I heroineize action along the line of faction,
Feeding my fish many times a day and

Petting my dog where he lie
On the bed beside my pillow,

No need for him to move
From where he furrows.

Boating on the lake,
Calling a good friend late,

No clean slate.

## Bridgeless

You look good to me. You look good to me.
From what I see, you look good to me.
From what I see, I think you should
Step aside, let me by; I'm coming through,
Going all the way—so step aside,
I'm coming to you and me, let it be,
Right or wrong, weak or very strong,
We can be our every dream about it all the time,
You and me walking free,
Going down Lovers Way it seems.
From what I see, you look good to me.

# I Knew You Would

Deep in my mind I knew you would
Call me as soon as you could.

I knew you would

Call me as soon as you could,
Deep in my mind I knew you would.

We met at another time
In different frames of mind.

Miles we've traveled to this point
To get to where we're at.

Play me like a drum.
Turn me around on your thumb.

I am yours.

Strum me and I am in key.
I am so engrossed when you sing with me.

Sing with me.

## Singing Softly

Singing softly—
Nobody's hearing our broken strings.

Won't you meet me by the fireside?
It's all been us looking back on time.
We've all been there in the stars sometime—
Few but a little still remember.

I think I love you and so I do,
Calling for you as I do.
I'm so happy to be with you,
Can't you tell I'm 'knowing' too?

Won't you meet me by the riverside?
It's not farther: light is still behind.
We've all seen them looking back in time—
Few stars a little still remember.

Becoming Familiar

Wonderful words are what we speak
As our ears hear each kiss on the cheek.

When your lips touch mine
I get this feeling inside;

It's like gracing a moth's wings
With my fingertips.

As dust it subsides
One kiss at a time.

## Minend

Come and get
What you're giving to me.

I've rented it out.
Now it's sold
To the one
That I believe

In your soul,
In you're mine, end.

You're the One

If you're looking for fun I am the one
To dance with under the stars or
Gaze at each other under the moon—
I'd like to get together soon.

I hold onto dreams and nap at noon—
I even sing songs of any tune.
With you by my side

It doesn't matter—what is time?
I'm good just knowing that you're mine.

## Lover Listeners

My one.
My lover forever.
My everyday.

You are my flower in the rain,
The sun on a cool evening
Setting as we stay.

Together we comfort one another;
Tears falling from nowhere,
Our arms serve as blankets

During nights of long-lasting twinkling stars
In eyes that have seen ways
Through the paths we've survived.

Now having reached destinations
We had only dreamed of in the past,
We encourage the other's heart to beat

In an everlasting-melodic resilience
Only the minds of lovers understand—
The importance of living forever

Within that song:
Ghosts' breathtaking whispers
Within the ears of lover listeners.

The Proposal

It's time to wake up now.
It's time to see the dreams we hold.
It's time for a new beginning,
Ours have grown old.

I need to think of ways to express my thoughts,
All jumbled they are when I talk.
Forward is a possible path,
Never looking back scared.

Our breadcrumbs have been eaten,
Our path with barefeet beaten,
We can find our way together,
No ties needed before forever.

## The Boat Ride

Let's not go too far too fast:
Let's not sink this ship we're in.

I'm not going to go anywhere:
I'm not going to leave your trail.

There's no end the future brings:
Let's make this boat ride last.

I'm going to go where you need me to:
I'm going to go where I say 'I do.'

Love Rhymes

You want to play games with me.
You want to make rhymes.
You want to change my name,
"It's only a matter of time."

One, two. You love me you say it's true.
Three, four. I love you, I love you even more.
Five, six. Let's not play these tricks.
Seven, eight. Just can't wait.
Nine, ten. Please say when.

You want to play games with me.
You want to make rhymes.
You want to change my name,
"It's only a matter of time."

## Love Rhymes, Too

"I love you."
'I love you too.'
"I love you three."
'I love you 4ever and again.'

Love Notes

I love you, you know it's true.
Got some things that I want to do with you—
Love me too.

## Possession

Your body
Is an amazing place
For me to roam:

With my hands
I've finally found a place
To call my own.

Cycles

Never have I loved another.
There is this feeling together:

We are lovers in an ever-setting sun,

Rise though everyday it does
As if dark never was.

# Creation

I have been creating a daydream and
You are in my mainstream.

All I do is think about you:
You are my night and daylight too.

Ocean and river waves
Only scape the depth of caves.

I sometimes anticipate thoughts
That are then spoken between the two of us.

Where we began, created by prospective
Deserts of dust and sand,

Where the rain of jungles spring cover for lovers—
Beneath the endless skies, that's where our love survives.

In the Morning


In the morning
Rambling on
I think of you
Until it's gone.

Hope and flowers,
Dreams come true—
All I could ever ask for,
Them all coming from you.

You on my mind makes life a boat ride.
Across the sea and desert sands
You are there holding my hand.

Great things are what I see
When I look into your eyes.
Your soul is there, no surprise.

Beautiful and bright,
Guided I am by the light.

# ¾ Song

Dance with me, waltz with me, do everything with me.
Rolling and strolling and playing around with me.
Eating stromboli, sharing that bowl with me,
Holding me tightly all alone with me.

Sitting alone with me on the porch we see
Hundreds of lights flashing, passing by you and me.
Feel the rain, it's coming down,
Watching the rainbow from the ground.

Catching love it lights up my life.
Making love is ever so nice.
Vices minor, never major:
Love is a song—the keys never change.

Finding the word there is no sound.
Here we go both on the ground.
Come with me, dance with me,
Spend your whole life with me.
Hold me tightly, 'Don't ever let go of me.'

Well here we are alone like before.
Joining is freedom and there's so much more.
Follow me, lead me, do what you please with me,
Holding me tightly, coming onto me.

## Breadcrumbs Forever

It's time I started listening to you—
It seems that's all my mind can do.
Everything that my eyes hold dear,
Everything I wish is here.

Come and hold me and lay me away,
Away my reserves are gone to stay.
Though my mind seems to wander,
Here you are: breadcrumbs forever.

Hear your whispers and the radio.
Oh baby, go real slow.
Life with love and the radio,
Us together moving slow.

## Crumbs

Imagine if I had no voice,
No voice to speak to you,
Limited in what I say,
But not in what I do.

Love Someone

When you love someone,
You're going to hurt someone.
Never let that stand in your way.

Never look at the future;
Let it go by real slow.
I guarantee you'll like it,

You'll see as you go.
Never look at the past.
Always have an open mind.

## With You

Sometimes I close
My eyes tight
So as not
To see another.

In such
I close you out
Of my vision
As well.

But when my eyes are open
I see what I have in you and
Do not need
In those staring back.

## Don't Go/Stay

Waiting on you to call is so hard to do.
I really do need to hear straight from you.
I lie awake at night wishing you were near.
I always and forever hold you in my heart so dear.

Please don't leave.
Please don't go.
I always want to know you and
How old we grow.

Your caress is what I long for,
Your voice so far away,
I need your touch to sleep at night:
It's no longer play.

Please don't leave.
Please don't go.
I always want to know you and
How old we grow.

## For You

The minutes tick slowly, my heart beats lonely.
My mind races, but as I wait for you
I know it's worth the pace.

Debt

With nothing much more to say
I place on hold my day.

With you in mind I think all the time
About what makes me happy.

The melody of life now comes at a very small price;
Paying only my debt to you with
Thoughts of love and gratitude.

## My Mine

You are the one, the entire measure,
The count that makes the song.

It's you with me
That makes things like this true.

No?


There is no poem or lyric,
No melody or dance,
No single word or expression
That would suffice in
Conveying the emotions
Within my heart and
Thoughts within my mind.

## Girlie's Jam

Working on finding you.
It is tough to do.
Can't you come calling, too?
Trying to deceive.
It is so hard to breathe.

Won't you sing to me?
Tell that I love thee.
It is not my time,
Seeing through
The scars you leave.

The book it bleeds,
With drops of ink
It beads.
I will find you.
Alone is where I will find you.

## Skipper's Lament

Please, I know you want to cut my hair.
I know you know I like it there.
Like the leaves falling down,
No longer do I care.
No longer do I care.

Please, won't you change my luck tonight?
Don't you want to make it right?
All you carry in the wind,
You know how long it's been.
It has been a long time.

I'll do my best to make your dreams come true.
You do your best to make mine come too.

Please, if you dream at all tonight,
Cut my hair and do it right,
Hair no longer in the wind,
It has been a long night.
You make it such a long night.

Looking in the coffee so brown,
Can't you tell that I'm around?
Calling for you to come 'round,
Drinking much more than my share,
I no longer see my hair.

Sentry

The ice that had kept my feet cold
Melted away only to freeze upon your step
Creating a new fold.

Within that deck we share,
Walking the same line with care,
Upon each other's eyes we stare,
Both wondering why and where

The same determination of which
Our fates and souls turn into gates
When and if that ice breaks,

In which direction it goes
Does not depend on fast or slow,

Weights on shoulders
Of one we know,
In control of movement,
Come or go.

On what side one takes to stand,
Open or closed,
Depends on the dealer, the offensive hand.

Yet still know
That the direction and depth of our fate
Is a two-way gate.

Fall Leaves

You are hurt and so am I.
How dare the fall leave us broken?
The remains, the shards:
A mirror smashed.

We gather together ever so carefully
Wanting to reassemble that which could
Cut our hands and bleed
Empty our hearts.

## In Moderation

Sorbet in the summer,
Whiskey in the winter:
I moderate myself
With your presence all year.

It comes about all the time
That I neglect you some,
But how am I to fulfill my life
When you're always gone?

Thinking that I lost your love.
Thinking that I lost your love.

I call on you to see if we can still survive.
The way we've been going there seems no other lie.
I've told you now, once before, the way it is today:
I will be here as long as you really want me to stay.

Thinking that I lost your love.
Thinking that I lost your love.

Someone

Like him!
So far away—unable to touch,
Too busy to respond,
Too famous to care about
*My* head in the crowd.

Like him?
Friend I already knew,
Too smart,
Too much of an ass,
I concede: this being the last.

Like him,
My lips wrinkle,
My eyes water through gritting teeth,
Two puppies lying at my feet,
What is it that I am to someone?

25

His hands turned me on:
They were a little rough and slightly injured.

His mind I did not know:
He nodded his head to my speaking.

Heavy my mind rests,
Holding this burden I might be crushed.

Young I wished only at heart—
His age the hell part.

Maybe it was my soul that made him look young.
Maybe it was his youth that was the turn on.

So In Love


I walk into you everyday.
Once a week I say 'Hi.'

I don't know what to do,
I don't know what else to say.

You smile at me this time.
You know I'm in love with you.
'I am so in love with you.'

I gave my heart away
Hoping it would go to use.

I'm so dependent
On knowing the truth.

You seem to love me.
Please tell me the words
"I'm so in love with you."

# Disposition

You are as cool as that night under the late autumn sky,
Yet you warm up with just a touch.

You are as smooth as coffee froth
As well as articulate, beautiful and sound—

Like a musical composition,
Yet you got lost in the crowd.

## Consideration

I want to be able to think of you before
I can't stop thinking about you.

## Blind Dates

You be a flake of snow
That melts upon my gaze,
Disappearing within—falling.

Cognates

At a loss I am for words
To describe how I feel.
I can't seem to formulate the truth,

Though as my mind searches
It's all around you.

I come to the conclusion
That us together
Makes my heart beat waves.

I don't want to repeat the pattern of the past.
I don't want to go too deep,

Yet as I continue to wade
Within your presence
I believe that all will eventually wash away

As tears to pain,
Responding like a hug to hurt.

## Time To Fly

Beautiful people—lyrics in the sky.
I just saw you, need I say 'Hi'?
It's all encompassing,
It's time to fly.
Where are all those people?
You're in my eye.

When I see you sweet melody is in my head.
Walking by we seek what it was that they had said.

Inquisitive people always asking why.
Where are all those words? Should I say 'Hi'?
It's all encompassing,
It's time to fly.
Here we go,
Don't ask why.

Many questions always asking why.
It's time to fly.
Where will we be next time it is that we say "Hi"?

You just saw me!
Please say "Hi."
It's all encompassing
It's time to fly.
Take my arm and hold me;
The umbrella's dry.

# I (Still) Think You're Number One

I ask myself, 'Is it really such a waste of time?'
Watching clouds go by, seeing images of you,
Is it really such a waste of time?

Crying for you—is it really such a waste of tears?
I think you're number one and a whole lot of fun.
Calling for you has got to be the right time.

This is what was said to me.
This is how it ought to be.
Now we can talk real free;
Please, won't you believe me?

I think to myself about our very, very, very next time,
Waiting for you to tell me just what to do,
There's no more wasting time.

This is what was said to me.
This is how it ought to be.
Now we can talk real free;
Please, won't you believe me?

I ask myself, 'Is it really such a waste of time?'
Watching clouds go by, seeing images of you,
Is it really such a waste of time?

I think you're number one and a whole lot of fun.

## Hometown Streets

One hand, two hands, ten fingers to count on.
One foot, two feet, hometown streets to walk down.

One, two, three, four, spring, summer, fall,
Winter is gone until next year.

Growing up is fun.
It's just being you,

Times it by the years you grow,
That's how life is you know.

The Last Sensation

Walk is long.
Forever your guide: the sky.
Proverbial strength within,
Sense of health declining,
Knowledge growing.

Daylight enters your mind.
Heart finds peace
As beating begins to diminish,
Conjectures wander,
Places to discover.

As in dream,
Connections open.
The crescendo—
Repetition, breathing depleting,
Rest.

## The Incinerator

Souls play on, on a melody
Before touching a bag of bones.

Lost soul finds oneself
Talking over skulls.

Thinking of two wispy souls
Wandering,

Wondering about conviction,
Vegatized, substantiating ideas

Of clubs and idols,
Careful to fight the grain

In nights of sleepilessness,
Knowing it would be best—adventurer—

To correct kicking quirks:
Deteriorating at the loss of another with

Loss of self.

## Semantics

Walked into a web, got dew on my head.
Oh, needy spider: your home is no longer stead.
Walk on.

Walked into a creek, got my feet in a little deep.
Said 'Thanks fish,' and drank what I wished.
Walk on.

Heard many deer rutting so near.
Laid low just so they'd know.
Walk on.

Walked to a field—felt the sun, oh it healed.
Wished to be found, oh feet walk the ground.
Walk on

To where gardens grow and red apples glow,
To where friends of friends now know.
Walk on. Walk on.

## Got Over the Rainbow

Follow the rainbow going to get it all someday:
Finding the pot of gold shining bright we know.
Working on this we're going to have to move
Real damn slow.

Moving along we go down the path we know.
Shooting for love our legs go weak below.

We've had enough of that looking forward/back.
Writing diaries in our heads we know that
Calming the soul has got to be the long way to go.
There's got to be another way to go.

Adventurer


You supported me
When I wasn't quite there.
I stayed at your house
As if it were my own.

Boating in January? Again soon?

Missing you when I am at home,
Missing shade even today
As fog lay heavy over the hill.

Do You Feel the Same?

I forgot that I planned to see you today.
Do you feel the same?
It's not memory,
It's déjà vu.
Do you feel the same?

Forgotten thoughts,
Maybe even dreams
Are catching up to us.
Not enough proof?
It's déjà vu.

It takes energy to survive.
Build your own life.
Forget-me-not flowers,
It's déjà vu.
Do you feel the same?

## Running Empty

Followed you through sick and sin.
Followed you to your door was always open.
Now that I'm no longer in the following you progression,
I wait until I can breathe again and sit in my recession.

You breathe like you have air to spare,
I guess it's not that way.
You think that you have things to share,
Well time has gone away.

I am where you thought I'd be:
An open book, I hope you enjoyed the read.
Never have I thought I would concede in your game.
Watch me as I walk away; you're not worth the pain.

I hope you no longer think that
I care about you so.
You pushed me as I walked away,
Your eyes were even closed.

Now that I no longer hurt,
I'm happy as it flows:
You've lost everything with me and
That's the way it goes.

Sock

If I were a sock
I would have been
Missed more.

Hungry?


It's been fun.
See you next time,
Next week,
Next year—
It's been like this too long.

## Dog Days

My mind opened for you and it closed just the same.
Pieces of love scatter my used heart—
No longer used: a breeze on a cool winter day.

Trying to close and lock spaces left empty
Filled with 'you thoughts,'
Loathing keeps the breeze from carrying away

That which doesn't know the difference
Between love of crossed bridges and
Love of trust.

## You Thoughts

Oh save me.
Save me from my mistake.

Oh save me.
Save me from my disgrace.

Your memory is a breeze on a cool winter day,
Yet that breeze does not carry you away.

As my heart is filled with 'you thoughts,'
Shivers run from bone to bone:

I do not feel creative.
I do not feel more than wasted—
Lost in 'you thoughts.'

## Pollen On My Feet

You be on my mind
Like a bee on a flower.

Though I am dressed to leave with pollen on my feet
That which remains keeps me pacing.

I want more, but I remember as
Your memory ensues,

As I move slow, here and there looking to gather more, and
Wishing you would stay and not wilt away,

That you are better off being
Like the flower.

## What's (Still) Inside?

It's that person that I ignored;
The one I can't face anymore.

In the mirror I stare and see all the hate
Looking back at me. When will I be free?

When your hand touches mine
How can I continue to cry?

Based on all that you say,
Forgiveness is the easy way

In the storms that I create—
I can't see beyond my mistake.

Running from myself at night,
Is it a dream or is it life?

How can I see the light
When my eyes are closed so tight?

What can I do?
That's right.

As you stand by my side
I find the simplest delights.

Trying to comprehend
Why you still want to be my man

I take another stand
Simply by holding your hand.

4ever


Being by your side I get why I'm alive.
Lost my way you say. Tears roll down your face.
As we touch each other's hands—pain is gone away.

Each time I see the look in your eyes returning my stare,
It's a flower in the sun returning every year.

Watching you as you see the mirrors in my eyes,
I might not be what you thought of me;
As I open the door you seem to adore me more.

## How Things Have Changed

My wheels were stolen; no one saw the way.
My lips were sealed, the message so far a way.
You waiting heard my call,
My heart was broken, but now not at all.

You in my life things have changed,
All that I've wanted, nothing's the same.
There are no games, but you play with me,
You wear your heart on your sleeve.
You wear your heart on your sleeve.

Sometimes in the night I hear you cry,
Tears of what you have so deep inside
Just for me as I look into your eyes,
No longer hurt, it's happiness in disguise.

## All About Tails

Cat tails feel like shark fins and
They're shushed away.

Mousetraps await a grand return,
Snaps still sprung.

Six lay dozens, breakfast forlorn,
Void of scraps, corn and clear-sunny days.

Stepping around moonlit splotches on the porch
I tip my smoke and

On quiet toes, now inside, scan for 'mere dog,'
Close in name to the fish,

Which is probably dozing in corners or
Asleep at the bottom, dreaming.

Who knows?
A fish's brain?

## Beyond Alternatives

'Breathe, fish in a bowl,
Take pills to survive or die.
Talk in code, please don't code.'

"This stream is not my home.
No way to breathe,
Please let me die in peace."

Bubbles they breathe for me; they are goldfish.

It took some time to understand that
Everything was not a dream.

What I've done to make you see; you're no slave to me,
It cost so much as you float belly up.

Bubbles they breathe for me; they are goldfish.

Four years and days gone by
You're still floating in my mind.

Took you from your hometown and
I put you underground.

Bubbles they breathe for me; they are goldfish.

## Coalbin Cat

Cat that would not pull back,
Talked along an echo
With its gallant kitty caller

Who unable to let go
Walked out the door again to hear
Calls from cat no more.

They now united
Entered the room
Where one dog lie near

Another dog's back
Under the bed of the
Coalbin Cat.

Please Recycle

In this place where my words have been restricted
To compliant tones for ears that hear them not,

I tweak what is even said
To fit the canal, yet it's all in vain as

The words fall dead.
I can't escape the sympathy that brings this all true.

My efforts and I are now being nibbled and
As bait swallowed I hold onto the belief that
I will neutralize what is digesting my soul.

In this place where my efforts get lost and I can't talk,
Where my eyes now only see the glow of
My own heart fading as

I become the one now consuming:
As a dream to another life living off rest.

As they awaken I dissipate into consciousness where
Repeated patters trample my efforts to survive then
I realize I've been awake this whole time.

## Never Knows?

Remembering yesterday
Tomorrow is a thought away

From today

Where weariness rests
Feeding on dreams.

Hazy

I've never seen so clear before,
Through the smoke, kin,
Blood of another

Running through my veins
From a person, one of which
I came, yet far in distance.

Mother,

You are a thought I think.
As you see me in old age,
As I have seen myself at that stage,

We are the same, some parts.
As you experienced the new form, a child once,
The ideas are similar:

I see you young, too at times,
As you see me old.

Daughter,


I did not have you.
You: you're even older than I am.
We understand, Mother?

I am your daughter, too.
Teach me your strength.
Daughter of mine, I did not have you, I did not have to.

## Perspective

You will never
See us in old age
As we have
Never seen you
As children.

## Stationary

Though it is not periodically time for an Indian Summer, such a period has occurred as I have come upon these years of my life.

Even as an idealist I realize that cold times crawl like sticky fingers through uncombed hair while the whitetail flags in fear, but I know that there are meadows in the brush, water on leaves and Indian Summers in the midst.

## Conceptual Existence

I think I am—
I think—
I am what?

Educate

Attend university
To get more diversity.

## Innate Communications

Do inanimate objects
Which contain energy and are sustenance to life

Understand the animate
The way time is understood?

With time being incomprehensible
There is strife for immediate truth and knowledge.

United in the entirety of one being,
Immediate communication might exist without time.

Herbivores

'Hey.'
"Hay is for horses."
'Not if it's spelled right.'

Recycle

Though with time,
Knowledge and expansion are gained.

Things do not merely die.
Energy is recycled and thoughts live on.

Thoughts and dreams/electrical impulses
Are preludes to chemical compounds.

Death is not the end of even one's own reality.

## Incomprehensible

With each concept,
Every religion and philosophy is in existence:

As an individual thinks of being created by a deity
So then they are.

Individuality exists only because it takes time
To communicate.

No time to gain gratification or communicate
Would result in lack thereof and total truth.

## Extrapolate

You probably just blew
Your own
Chances at gratification.

Q: Where did the sinner have lunch?
A: The confessional stand.

"Why do you have a potato chip on your shoulder?"
'It's Halloween and yes, I have a chip on my shoulder.'

## Synopsis

Deities conceptually exist as
Time is incomprehensible.

Intrinsic knowledge is on delay because
It takes time to communicate.

If time could be attained,
Yielding inherent knowledge,

The single entity that is
Would be understood.

Closing mind,
Closing mind.

# About the Author

E. I. Karnes resides in Pennsylvania and graduated from Penn State University with a baccalaureate from the College of Communications in Journalism.

This author is a visual artist and enjoys working with various mediums, likes music, kayaking and volunteers time helping to create and maintain an ecologically diverse and recreationally-friendly environment.